a

The Dishes Are Done Man!

book

BOOKS BY *Lacey Noonan*

NOVELLAS

A Cruzmas Carol: Ted Cruz Takes a Dickens of a Constitutional

Seduced by the Dad Bod: Book One in the Chill Dad Summer Heat Series

Hot Boxed: How I Found Love on Amazon

The Babysitter Only Rings Once

I Don't Care If My Best Friend's Mom is a Sasquatch, She's Hot and I'm Taking a Shower With Her ...Because It's the New Millennium

I Don't Care if My Sasquatch Lover Says the World is Exploding, She's Hot But I Play Bass and There's Nothing Hotter Right Now Than Rap-Rock ...Because It's the New Millenium (Book 2)

Eat Fresh: Flo, Jan and Wendy and the Five Dollar Footlong

A Gronking to Remember

A Gronking to Remember 2: Chad Goes Deep in the Neutral Zone

The Blacker the Robot the Moister the Oyster: Falling for the Obamacare Sex Robot (My Obamacare Nightmare Book 2)

NOVELS

Shipwrecked on the Island of the She-Gods: A South Pacific Trans Sex Adventure

COLLECTIONS

The Hotness: Five Burning Hot Novellas

The Nasty Woman's Guide to Deplorable Baskets

PRAISE FOR *A GRONKING TO REMEMBER*

"We were made aware this weekend that Gronk erotica exists and is being sold on Amazon. Due journalism diligence insisted we purchase this Gronk erotica, give you a full review, and then turn it into an animated movie."

—Deadspin

"'Lacey Noonan,' an author—nay, an American hero—recently penned one of the greatest works of fan fiction we here at Complex Sports had ever seen… We're talking highbrow shit here."

—Complex

"It's been a slow year for people who have been looking for NFL-related erotica novels, but the drought is finally over thanks to author Lacey Noonan (Not pictured above)."

—CBSSports.com

"Rob Gronkowski might just be the hero that the world of erotica needs right now."

—Inquisitr.com

"Rob Gronkowski Erotica Is Here and It's… Something."

—Boston.com

"The western canon is scattered with watershed works of literature penned by American authors…add A Gronking to Remember to that list."

—Brenden, amazon reviewer

"I don't want to live in a world where this book doesn't exist."
—David B. Hansen, *amazon reviewer*

"Thought this was going to be about the hash browns at Dunkin' Donuts. Disappointing!"

—happykins, amazon reviewer

Dark

Desires:

Taken by the Obamacare Sex Robot

My Obamacare Nightmare Book 1

LACEY NOONAN

ISBN: 1539723666
ISBN-13: 978-1539723660

Special Thanks

George Washington, Thomas Jefferson, James Madison, Benjamin Franklin, Thomas Paine and all you other big time ballers in scraggly wigs and tight pantaloons…

CONTENTS

To America

Dark Desires

America will never be destroyed from the outside. If we falter and lose our freedoms, it will be because we destroyed ourselves.
—Abraham Lincoln

I don't want your freedom.
—Wham!

CHAPTER ONE

A Perfect Day

The Obamacare sex robot couldn't have come at a worse time.

Look, even though I'm a conservative and adhere to the notion that this country has gone *way* off track, I'm not one of those high maintenance wives who gets her panties in a bunch over the littlest, most meaningless things—living in a gated Connecticut neighborhood, I was surrounded by these women— but having a goddamned *pleasure cyborg* delivered by the United States Postal Service right in the middle of my very first baby shower... It was like a slap in the face.

A slap I tell you.

Salmon pink, baby blue and eggshell streamers hung from the ceiling of our sun porch. The white wicker chairs had been aligned in a semi-circle for days. And balloons, balloons, balloons! Balloons everywhere. So many balloons of all shapes and sizes, the room looked like a county fair.

My mother and I had been planning the baby shower for weeks, our lives a tizzy of decorations, teas and little cakes. We'd spent a small fortune on invitations. Every day of planning the paper quality seemed to get better, thicker, more deckled, and the lettering more gilded and italic.

"Come on guys, how much of my salary is going into this?" my husband Bradley complained one evening after dinner, and my mother retorted with such a ferocity that it nearly knocked me off my kitchen island chair:

"This is my *first* grandchild, *your* first child and there is no price too pricey, so man up, Brad-Brad!" she exhorted.

At that, Bradley slowly backed out of the room, smiling, hands raised in the air in surrender.

I laughed—I'd never really been able to argue with Bradley's money concerns. It was *on* after that. (Speaking of county fairs) my mother found a service that rented baby lambs for events. We went to look at him at his farm and I could *just* picture him baaing and wandering through our backyard in a yellow bow. The little guy was *so* cute and *so* fluffy… I had to admit, as I rested my hands on my growing baby bump, I was really looking forward to my baby shower. It was going to be *perfect*. Perfection: the word rang clear in my mind, like a heaven of clean and white clouds, uncolored by any shadow or dark, nasty dirtiness. Perfection is a world unto itself. Nothing not wanted gets in. And only those of your kind—the best kind.

Finally, the day arrived.

One by one, the ladies came. Friends, family—flowerily dressed, behatted in huge, round hats as big as sombreros absolutely *smothered* in lavender and pink taffeta and lace. The sun porch filled to capacity. It was so amazingly heartwarming to have so many women come support me on my journey. Motherhood is an honor. I was honored to have so many women honoring me so.

I didn't fight her. I slipped my body with its round belly into the outfit my mother had picked out for me: a Tiffany Rose maternity dress, sleeveless, with crossover neckline and bright, colorful poppy pattern and jersey sash that separated my blooming breasts and stomach with a dash of deep, conservative red. It seemed everything on the front of my body had quintupled in size and roundness. I hadn't been able to wear my heels for weeks now, so I slipped my weary tootsies into a pair of Tory Burch ballerina flats.

My mother was a frenzy of hugs and directions and small talk, saying, "Now, now, Edna or Lisa or Bernadette, Holly *doesn't* want to *hear* your *horror* stories," whenever one of the older moms leaned in with her birth story of endless agony and twilight

16

drugs of the 1970's.

We were in a cool-down period between events when the doorbell rang. I'd already opened the gifts, stacked all over the house. Baby monitors, toys, diapers. In a few minutes we'd get to the games. Tea was served by the catering staff, a multicultural yet mostly dark-hued bunch. While I didn't approve of slavery, as was the correct way to think about such things these days, there was a subtle harmoniousness that day to the mathematical balance of the sheens of server and served. Slanted, golden sunlight filled the room. It was a spring morning, cool and beautiful. Fine china clinked. Tea sipped. Scones munched. Outside, the baby sheep bleated. My friend Bethany named him Leroy. Leroy the Lamb.

"I love you, Leroy!" shouted Bethany through the window.

I laughed. We were sitting in the corner of the sun porch. I needed a rest. I was exhausted, like a gift card.

"Oh *my God*, I'm *so* jealous of you right now, Holly. I miss being pregnant *so* bad, so very totes bad," she said, and rubbed me on the stomach like I was a magic lamp. "Is he kicking much? Keeping you up at night?"

"I—"

"Oh my God, Aiden and Jayden and Rayden kept me up *all* night. Oh my God, you have no idea. Like full-on karate kicks!" Bethany roared and leaned back, her huge body shaking, smiling at her own joke, if you could call it that.

"The doct—"

"What hospital are you going to again?"

"Hartford Institute of—"

"Oh, thank *God*," she said, disdain suddenly rippling on her round face, her skin pasted with thick makeup. Bethany could be a super bitch when she wanted to be—'Bethany the Bully'—which is why we loved her. She was big and round. Not fat—just formidable—built like an ATM. I think she threw discus in high school, though she still dressed like a teen model with the body of a triple-jumper, exposing everything in revealing and see-through clothes whenever she could, like the sheer Lane Bryant princess dress she wore that I think was meant to be a slip. "Those homebirth hussies at New Haven Midwifery tried to get their paws on us, but we stood firm. I mean, what the hell? I want drugs and I want a *doctor* there if anything goes wrong!"

"Yeah—"

"I mean forget it! Drug me up! Knock me out! I don't wanna feel a thing!" Bethany screamed in my face. "Epidural my ass up!"

"My thirty eight week appointment is tomorrow," I was finally able to get in edgewise. "Or wait, I think it's Tuesday…"

"Preggo brain!" Bethany shouted, squeezing my hand, hurting me. I had the sudden feeling that she wanted to eat me, but the feeling passed.

I laughed. "Well, either way, it's this week. So yeah. We'll find out if everything's okay and we can go ahead and schedule the C-Section."

"Hells yeah!" Bethany roared.

Then, ding dong…

Across the house the doorbell rang. People had been filing in for hours now, so I didn't think anything of it.

About a minute later, the entire party went silent. "Is everything okay?" I asked from my wicker chair.

I heard my mother's voice quaver from the living room. "I think you better come in here, Holly," she said. With Bethany's help, I struggled from my chair and waddled into the living room.

"I'm so sorry, Holly," she said. She was crying.

"What? What is it, mother?"

"I thought it was a big gift being delivered, I thought, I…" she trailed off into tears. My Aunt Bernice steadied her, held her arm. "Easy, Gayle," she said. "Easy now, woman."

I looked down. It was a giant wooden crate, almost as big as a coffin, sitting in our living room.

When I saw what was written on the side I screamed as if stabbed.

CHAPTER TWO

The Hornswoggling of America

Bradley flew into the room. We'd heard his feet tromping in the rooms above where he was hiding, then flying down the stairs.

"What!? What is it!" he was yelling, "Where's Holly? Is it time? Is it time?"

I was sprawled on the couch, tears in my eyes. "How could you?" I said to Bradley through the tears and through the booger snot.

"How could I *what?*" he said.

"Look!" I yelled, pointing.

The women parted to reveal the wooden crate. On the side it read: *Affordable Care Act Bx-44 Gratification System — Property of United States of America.*

"A damned Obamacare Sex Robot!" I yelled and dissolved into swampy tears.

"At our baby shower!" said my mother.

"In your house!" Aunt Bernice chimed in.

Bradley went red in the face. He flexed his muscles, the veins on his neck popping out. He exercised a lot, kept his body in great shape, so it was kind of scary to see. He was suddenly piping mad. "I didn't order this! Is this a joke? Who sent this? Is this a joke?" he sputtered, looking around the room. "I'm calling the post office—No, I'm calling the police! This is a joke! Fucking, Obama! This is Obama's America now. Force shit on you you don't want!"

Women stood back from Bradley's masculine fury. He pulled out his phone and disappeared into the kitchen.

Meanwhile, the opinions in the room had reached consensus…

"My cousin Edwina's husband ordered one through Medicaid," one of my mother's friends named Annette whispered. "He was down at the club when it was delivered, so she opened the box. Opened it right up. Looked just like Edwina!"

"No!"

"Only it wasn't just Edwina. It was Edwina *thirty-five* years younger. They make them to order.

Her husband said he *needed* it. Said Edwina wasn't satisfying his *needs* any more. Like a sixty-five year-old man's needs is what makes the world go round. What more does an old fart need besides golf and looking at his dividend statements?"

"Tsk tsk."

"And he said it wasn't an affair because it was a robot—like using an electric toothbrush to brush your teeth."

"No!"

"They say it's the new Viagra™, these sex robots…"

"All free of charge. The bill footed by the American tax payer of course."

"I am happy that my husband has another avenue to unload his masculine desires, but nothing *we* need is ever free is it? All the abortions I want… free of charge. All the food stamps. All the homosexual starter kits. But then again, I guess hardworking, honest Americans have always had it hard and always will."

"It's an abomination."

"Obamacare is."

"*Damn* straight, Martha."

"Oh, that Obama in the Oval Office… He's a Muslim you know."

"Isn't he the worst?"

"Blech!" Bethany expectorated into the convo. Hers was the only voice I recognized with my head in my hands, my thoughts in disarray. "Barack *Hussein* Obama, you mean."

"Born in Africa. *Imagine.*"

"Kenya they say."

Someone whistled. "*Kenya?* Where is that?"

"*Africa.*"

"Good *Lord.*"

"I mean, it's *not* because he's black. I know tons of great ones. Down at the club... I mean, yes they work there... do an okay job, I *sup*pose—but there's that other one—oh, what's his name—the lawyer? Doctor something? He's one too. He's so nice."

"What the—pardon my French—*heck* is going on in this country? Nine eleven, then we elect a Muslim president. We're going to heck in a hand basket. Heck in a hand basket! I can't wait until we have someone sensible in office again. A big, strong cock-of-the-walk Caucasian man to lead us just like Ronald Reagan. I mean, this *Nobama...*"

"Not my president."

"Not my president."

"Not my president."

"Ladies, ladies!" Bradley addressed us, coming back into the room. He held up both hands. "I am sorry for this. No one's more pissed about this than me. This *thing* is going back. I just looked at our application on that godawful Obamacare website and there it is. You have to click a button to *opt out* of the program. First they made us sign up for this fascist free communist Nazi healthcare and then they make you get a... robot if your wife's pregnant. What a bunch of horse hockey! Ladies, we were hornswoggled. Talk about the hornswoggling of America!"

No one hated websites more than old women, so Bradley was preaching to the choir. "Ladies, please resume your party. I will deal with this," he said, coming into the room and kissing me on the forehead. "I love you, Holly, honey!" Then he grabbed the crate and dragged it out of the room and into the garage.

"Now that's a *real man*. A *good* husband," Aunt Bernice said and the party got back to as normal as we could make it after such a terrible intrusion by Barack Hussein Obama's disgrace of a socialist healthcare system.

Later that night, after the party, after everyone—even my straggling mother and an even stragglier Bethany, drunk as a skunk on the signature cocktail Cucumber Mojitos and accidentally touching everyone's boobs on purpose and trying to ride Leroy the Lamb and only slipping on his poop and landing in a bush until I had to call her husband Graham to come get her—had left, Bradley and I sat in the porch talking. Bradley had a protein shake and I my nightly after-dinner 1/4th of a glass of pinot grigio that I savored more than life itself.

"Look, I need to call Obamacare and sort this out," Bradley said. "Do you mind going to the doctor's appointment alone tomorrow? You know how long they keep you on hold at healthcare.gov. Those dot gov *fascists*. And then I can go down to the strawberry farm and get some work done."

Naturally, like everyone else, our lives had been living hells since the Obama Administration took over after Bush. Higher taxes, the Financial and Housing Crisis he'd caused thanks to the welfare state, welfare mothers and crack mothers, homosexual weddings jammed down our throats like… homosexual weddings, abortion clinics on every street corner, the repeal of the Second Amendment, Solyndra, the Acorn thingy, the fiascos in Afghanistan, Iraq, Benghazi, wherever that was, ISIS, PRISM, NAFTA, letting Snowden escape to Russia, all that liberal whining climate change mumbo-jumbo, and worst of all: *Obamacare*—otherwise known as The Affordable Care Act, with its Death Panels and enforced premiums, unconstitutional fines and its Sex Robots.

"Well… It's an important appointment," I said, sipping my drinky drink. "It will be long too. A couple hours. You gonna leave me alone for two hours?"

Bradley grumbled for a second. "I hate seeing you naked in front of the woman doctor. There, I said it."

"What? Really?"

"It makes me uncomfortable, Holly. Like I was sitting in a women's bathroom or something. Like I'm a voyeur or a perv like those, you know, whatever people. I know it's not happening that way, but it makes me think of lesbians for some reason, your legs spread open and the doctor's hand up there. I mean, why would a woman become a doctor? Why would she *really*, you know what I mean? Your vagina all open like that. Your *vagina*." He shivered. When he saw my frowning reaction, he quickly added: "I mean, I like knowing I have you all to myself, Holly! Like you're my property! Hidden away from the world."

I smiled. "I *am* your property, Bradley. I'm yours, I'm all yours. And when this kid pops out of me, he'll be yours too. Another McQuerty. Heir to the McQuerty throne!"

Bradley snickered and held me close.

I nuzzled into his hard body. I have to admit, I was feeling a little turned on. His smoky man-smell wafted down and mesmerized my senses. I wondered if his smell was more potent because he was so angry before. Did angry men turn women on? Probably. "So, you're not mad about *not* having sex all these months?" I asked.

"What? No. It's only natural. Frankly, it's been great for me," he said. "All that extra energy I can put into working out at the gym. I've never felt better." And he flexed his bicep muscle right before my eyes.

"Mmm," I said and slid my hand down Bradley's front. I went for the bulge in his navy blue Abercrombie & Fitch shorts. "So big and strong. What do you say we take this party upstairs and work on our downstairs?"

"Look, no. *Ew*, you're *pregnant*. I don't want the head of my dick knocking against Bradley Junior's head, you know," he said and pulled my hand away.

"But the doctor said it was okay," I said. "Even beneficial."

"That lesbo!" shouted Bradley. He laughed. I laughed too. "That's what pisses me off about this whole *Gratification System*," he said. "That the government thinks they know what's best for us. They think that just because my wife's pregnant that I need this robot to please me because she can't perform sexually."

"But, I want—"

"That you can't perform just because you're pregnant!"

"But—"

"That they think just because you're huge and fat now in the body and fat in the face and your ass is like two huge vats of cottage cheese that a husband doesn't want to have sex with you!" he said.

"But…"

"The nerve of that Muslim African basketball president saying my wife is ugly now! Health? Science? They call that science? Science is the workout I do down at the gym, getting my male body strong and shapely, getting those gains. It's like they want us to be *slaves*. Can't wait until they outlaw gyms! Man, I'd like to just get Obama in a room alone for five minutes. I'd show him what a *real* American looked like."

I had to admit it: Bradley was right.

"No, you're right. You're absolutely right," I said, nuzzling in to Bradley, unaware of the invisible gears of history grinding on us like a booty dancer grinding on a guy at a dance club.

CHAPTER THREE

Glistening More Glisteningly

Next morning, I was halfway to the obstetrician's office when my iPhone did its xylophone noise thing.

At the next stop sign I looked down and saw a Google Calendar alert on the screen. It was a reminder, notifying me that my appointment was for tomorrow morning at 10:30 AM. *Tomorrow.*

"Holly, you jerk!" I said, slapping my forehead. I turned around in a driveway and headed for home.

Twenty minutes later, I pressed the opener and pulled my Lexus LX SUV with black leather interior inside the garage. I exhaled. Turned off the car. It would be better this way... Bradley would give the healthcare.gov goblins a piece of his mind today, and so could come with me to the doctor's tomorrow. I looked down at the Sex Robot crate where Bradley had left it yesterday, sneering at it, the governmental waste of it.

"That's strange," I said.

Something was odd about the box. I trundled out of the SUV with my heavy girth, shut the door and walked over to the crate.

The wooden crate—the Obamacare Gratification System crate—was open. I moved the cover with my foot. It was empty! Just dark gray foam where a body had once been.

My jaw dropped. My clutch purse fell to the garage floor as I stepped back. I brought both hands up to my open mouth slowly. I was suddenly scared. Oh my God, I thought, looking around. What if this *thing* got out? What if it had attacked someone? Killed someone? What if it killed Leroy the Lamb? Or done *unnatural* things with Leroy the Lamb? More unnatural than Bethany? Who knows what kind of trouble this robot could get into. But then I thought: But it's a woman, right? What damage could a woman do? And what did she look like, this sex robot? Was it me? Thirty-five years younger? Thirty-five years ago I was negative seven years old. Was she naked, whoever she was? The police would pick her up—pick *me* up. Arrest *me*. I had so many questions. So many stupid questions I would not have had to answer if a worthless *liberal schmiberal* hadn't been elected to president a bunch of years ago.

I run-walked into the house, my girth swaying. I was about to yell for Bradley when I heard the telltale noise…

Creaking.

The kitchen ceiling was creaking, repetitively, above my head.

Our bedroom was above the kitchen.

I crept to the foot of the stairs. The creaking was less audible here, but something *else* was more audible…

The sounds of lovemaking. The sounds of lovemaking oozed across my eardrums like K-Y Jelly on a hot tin roof.

"No!" I grimaced. "No!"

Sex sounds! Oh my God, Bradley was fucking that sex robot after all. That liar! Oh my God, I'm going to take that liar for everything, I said to myself. Everything he owns! Divorce! My very soul screamed out for *Le Divorce!*

Oh yes, oh yes! *Oui, oui!*

I struggled up the stairs with my baby weight.

My blood pounding in my temples. There were so many stairs and I was already out of breath after five of them, but the hot wind of anger inflated me up the steps like I was a hot air balloon.

The sounds of bodies slapping got louder the closer to the bedroom I got. The door was closed. How so very respectful of Bradley to close the door, I thought, or possibly said out loud, I wasn't sure—crazed, I was crazed, hormonal, fat, in the face and the body—that scum, that liar, that lying scum liar!

"You said we were hornswoggled," I railed in the hallway in front of our bedroom door. "Hornswoggled! But *you* hornswoggled *me*. You hornswoggled me, Bradley McQuerty!" I flung open the bedroom door. "Oh my God! What the—!?!?!?"

I froze in my tracks.

The sight before me shocked me to my very core—the inedible part where the seeds are.

What froze me?

Please let me paint the scene I witnessed in the bedroom for you, because it really bears a full description. So strange, so very strange. Like a porno shoot. I hadn't watched much pornography in my life of course, I was a woman, but I'd seen enough by accident to know what was a classic porno set up and what wasn't. Well, this certainly *was…*

On the bed, my husband was on all fours, his ass high in the air, his head face down in the quilt. He was naked. He was very naked and moaning in ecstasy, low, full-bodied moans I'd never heard him make before, except maybe playing tennis? He must not have heard me yelling on the stairs or opening the door because he was moaning so loud. His body was shiny with sweat and he was rocking forward and backward, doggy style.

The strangest part of the scene, though, you'll surely agree, was Barack Obama.

Barack Obama was fucking my husband Bradley in the ass on our king sized bed. I couldn't believe it. I came in screaming, but when I witnessed the scene, my jaw dropped it like it's hot. I froze in place, as if paused in time by a magic spell.

I watched with horror as the president gripped Bradley by each hip and pumped his rock hard dick into him. Their bodies slapped together in sexual rhythm. Bradley's butt-cheeks rippled with the pounding, his skin rippling like the surface of water.

The president slid into him and lifted my husband ever so slightly from the bed, the better to penetrate him. He drew it out slowly, ever so slowly, then rammed it back deep into my husband's asshole. A light squishing sound percolated in my ears: the sound of Barack Obama's penis invading my husband Bradley's sphincter.

The grunting too.

So much grunting.

So much grunt work.

My eyes burned. The hairs on my neck stood on end. Barack Obama slapped Bradley on the ass while he fucked him and Bradley let out a warbling moan of pain and pleasure, raising his butt up a little more to take it—to take it good like a good boy. "Yes, Mr. President, pound my asshole, I'm your little bitch," he moaned.

So many conflicting emotions exploded inside me at once. I was a Big Bang of Emotional Fireworks: confusion, anger, surprise, shock, sadness. All the big ones, all the majors were there. Repulsion. Fear. Horror. A strange twinge of naughty titillation too. (It *was* sex after all. It had been soooo long since Bradley and I'd had any kind of intimacy because of my pregnancy.)

And really—two fit men going at it. Kind of hot. But mostly "What-the-Fuck-ness" was the high order of the day.

Then Barack Obama saw me!

He looked up and smiled, but continued to work my husband's hole like a true stud.

"I believe we have company," the president leaned forward and whispered into my husband's ear, nibbling on it, and continuing to slide his meat into the man in my life. Obama straightened up and addressed me, in a hollow mechanical version of that pretentious and messianic tone of his that he uses in speeches. "Would you like to join in, Mrs. McQuerty? Cup the balls, perhaps?"

Bradley shot up. He screamed when he saw me: "Ayyeee!"

I jolted from my trance. Jumped in my shoes.

Bradley unslurped his butthole from the president's cock. He rolled off the bed and crouched down behind it on the other side, hiding his nudity from me like Adam and Steve from God in the Garden of Eden.

"W-w-w-w-w-w-what the hell happened to your lesbo-gyno appointment? Were you *lying* to m-m-me?" Bradley machine-gunned, peering over the top of the quilt.

I was speechless. My husband was attacking *me* like *I'd* done something wrong. I had no answer, just stared dumbfounded at the whole scene. I began to back out the door. Then took a step forwards. Then back again.

The presidential sex cyborg coughed—a little sputtering of gears. I looked at him. He looked at me, then he looked down at Bradley. "I'm sorry to see your flaccidity has returned," the POTUS said and sat back against the headboard—my headboard—fully nude, his dark skin and even darker dick just, like, right *there*.

"Shut the fuck up, Obama!" Bradley screamed. "Get the fuck out of here, will you?" he then screamed at the both of us.

"Obama? Barack… Obama!?" I managed to say. How I was able to say anything at that point was a gosh darned miracle. I was still in shock.

But slowly I came out of it. I looked at Bradley, still behind the bed.

"Bradley…" I whispered. "What's going on? What's…"

"Get the hell out of here, will you, Holly! Everybody out!"

This really snapped me out of it. My anger won over the other emotions. "What the fucking heck, Bradley! Are you gay now? You're not a homo! Oh my God! Are you!?" I covered my open mouth with both of my hands. I started to swoon. My whole world was crumbling around me.

"It's a change we can all believe in," Obama said. His cock glistened, sticking straight up from his lap like a thick black flag pole. Glistening, it should be noted, with my husband's butt juices. I tried not to look, but it was *right there*.

"Shut the fuck up, Obama-bin-Laden!" Bradley yelled at Obama, semi-convincingly, as if Bradley had a leg to stand on. I wanted to run away, but I was locked in place, locked by my need to know the truth.

"Bradley! Did you at least you use lube?" I said. I shook my head, not sure why I'd asked that. It was one of those weird things you say when you can't believe the whole situation, so you focus on some trivial detail.

Bradley got up. "Yes! No! What! This fucking robot *forced* itself on me. I was— I was—" He grabbed a bunch of clothes and ran to the bathroom.

"I'm self-lubricating," Barack Obama said in an even voice, smiling at me. "Here, watch."

"Ew! God! No!" I shouted, looking away for a second, but then curiosity getting the best of me, I looked back and there it was. Obama's penis glistened in the soft morning light more glisteningly.

Then it hit me. *Robot had forced itself…?*

"Wait, what? *He* is the Obamacare Sex Robot?" I shouted at Bradley, "An Obama? You ordered an Obama!?"

"It's not a *he*, it's an *it*," Bradley yelled from the bathroom. "And I most certainly did not order that thing! It was for *you*, you *bitch*." He came out of the bathroom, dressed in his gym clothes.

"Bradley, you liar-fag!" I shouted. "Get out of this house immediately! Get out, *get out*, GET OUT!"

I picked up a table lamp and hurled it at him. He yelled and ducked.

The lamp smashed against the wall. The sound was incredibly satisfying. So incredibly satisfying in fact that I ripped the alarm clock off the table and threw it at him too. I threw like a girl, but this time I made contact. The clock slammed against his head, made a most pleasant thudding noise. He yelped in pain and fell back against the dresser.

"What the hell, Holly?" he said. He touched his hand to his head and there was blood on it. He looked at me, said, "What the hell?" again, this time with rising anger in his voice. He stepped towards me. He raised his fists.

I stepped backward.

"God damn you, you stupid, ugly worthless whore! I'm going to kill you!" He screamed and lunged at me. I screamed too.

But before Bradley could get to me, the Obama robot made some beeping noises and leaped from the bed, long dark democratic dong deviously dangling, and threw a nasty right hook into Bradley's face. Crack!

I couldn't believe what was happening.

This was all so CRAZY!

Bradley crumpled. He whimpered from the floor, his hand on his chin. He looked up at the Obama thing, then me, utter hatred glowing in his eyes. Then he ran from the room crying and fell down the stairs. Obama sat down on the side of the bed. A minute later I heard Bradley's car tearing out of the driveway.

Chapter Four

The Strawberry Farm

It wasn't even that good of a copy. They really could have tried harder. The eerie uncanniness you were supposed to feel was easily undermined by idle observation. If you looked close at the robot you could tell something was off about it, that it didn't match up with the man you saw *ad nauseam* a thousand million times a day on the news and in the newspapers. The robot lips were a little fuller. The nose bigger. The head rounder. The ears not sticking out as much. The hair was obviously synthetic, some kind of Astroturf, but looked softer than puppy fur.

Not that I knew what the president looked like naked, but I didn't think he was *that* muscular. I knew he played basketball and stuff because he was from the inner city of Chicago, but this robot's body defied credulity. He was *too* cut. He had the body of a twenty-year old male model. The biceps were too round. His chest sculpted as if from marble, with two perfectly round nipples like dark gold coins adorning it. His stomach flat, the abdominal muscles on it sharp and defined. His synthetic chocolate-colored skin glowed in the sunlight that streamed through the window as if enhanced with CGI. He was hairless and smooth. Not to mention its manhood… I tried not to look, but it was impossible not to. Not with a little dark throb deep inside me did I realize that this pleasure bot was *hung*. He had double the dick of Bradley.

No. Whoever had built this thing (and thought it was actually *okay* to send someone a replica of the president) built this thing poorly. They had gilded the lily (the lily-livered president), and made this thing the fantasy version of reality.

Not that I was *at all* interested in the Sex Robot for "what it was built for," but it was just another clear example of the poor craftsmanship of our government agencies. You wouldn't have been able to tell an "Open Market" Gratification Sex Robot from the real thing is all I'm saying.

Not that I cared one lick for the whole deal.

Not that I cared about this replica of Barak Obama, this built-for-pervy-pleasure-thingie, sitting stark naked on the side of my bed, hands on his knees as if he were waiting to get a haircut, erection erect, eyeballing me creepily.

"Is it safe to conjecture that you are entering your 39th week?" the Obamacare Sex Robot asked me. "Is that correct? Your due date is not synced with my files. I have not been set up with access to your Wi-Fi yet. Would you like a perineal massage?"

"Gross, Obama! No!"

I flew from the room. Slammed the door behind me.

My thoughts were all in wild disarray, like a hundred tiny blue racquetballs hit at once in an indoor racquetball court, the kind with the glass walls.

When the balls finally settled in their glass room, the first tiny blue thought that I picked up was not helpful: *I need to call Bradley—He'll know how to fix this.* That was my first thought—unhelpful to the Max. To the TJ Maxx, Fury Road.

I waddled downstairs into the kitchen. I was starving. I was pregnant. Do the math. I tore into leftovers from the shower. Cheese, crackers, crudités, canapés. I sat down at the kitchen island and scarfed it all down.

Ten minutes later, all the leftovers were gone (which was fortuitous, because it would be my last meal for a long, long time). My stomach gurgled. Suddenly, like bile, a rage came up into my throat. Bradley. BRADLEY. That turd! Gay or not, he was *holding out* on me all this time. He'd impregnated me in the first place, the least he could do was prime the doorway for the entrance of his child. I needed answers. I didn't care about the etiquette—who was supposed to call who when one discovers their partner with a glistening coital android—pretty sure Anne Landers didn't have a chapter on *that one*—though, who knew these days—life was getting crazier and more weird every day—the Obama Administration opening the door and letting all the fricking *weirdos* in—the door of the future like the Hellmouth or when that dick-less dude from Ghostbusters turns off the power of the ghost jail in the basement of the fire station in lower Manhattan and unleashes Hell... Ugh. See?—A thousand tiny blue racquetballs.

I went into the garage and retrieved my phone

from the floor where I'd dropped it. Shaking like a maniac crackhead, I started to dial Bradley's number, but the phone was already ringing. It was Bradley calling me. I answered.

"Don't say it," he said curtly, mean.

"Don't say what?"

"Don't say it. That's *all* I'm saying."

"Bradley, don't say what?"

"Just *don't* say it. Don't be obvious and say the obvious thing."

"Okay, *I won't.* Jesus. *Whatever* the hell you're taking about. Just talk to me. Please talk to me. Does this mean you're a Democrat now?"

"I SAID DON'T SAY IT!!!" Bradley screamed so loud I had to hold the phone away from my ear. "God damn you, Holly, you bitch!" There was all sorts of static noise.

I began to cry, to sob and blubber into the phone. Words like 'gaywad' and 'your baby' and 'obamacare sex robot' and 'how could you, you cheating Democrap bastard' came tumbling out.

"Let me cut you off there, Holly. Because I'm coming home. I'm on my way now. Now."

"Good."

"No, listen. I'm serious, *listen.* I can't fight it any more. Listen to what happened. This is

Obama's America now and I'm fine with it. Obama *won*. This sex robot delivery was the last straw. First my plumbing supply business goes out of business because of high taxes, then a Chinese hacker hacked my app, stole all my code, all the code I'd paid Bangladeshi coders to make for two hundred dollars and the government did nothing about it. But I still had my Strawberry farm right?"

"Had?"

"*We* still had it, right? Good old American strawberries made here in good old American Connecticut! But guess what Holly? And this is a laugh... you gotta laugh HA HA! It's gone now too! Fuck it! I don't care! I don't care anymore. I get down here to the farm to relax and think about stuff after what you did to me in the bedroom and the place is crawling with feds. They're foreclosing on it because they say I'm refusing to hire enough ethnic people, that I haven't hired any al-Qaeda-ass Syrian refugees. It's gone, Holly. The strawberry farm is gone too. I can't fucking fight it, Holly! I give in. I'll do anything to get stay on my feet. Even if it means sucking the Obamacare Robot's dick every morning, afternoon and night. So I'm coming home, Holly. Get ready. Get ready for the *new order*. The sanctity of marriage be damned, I'm about five minutes away. I'm coming home and we're going liberal!"

The phone fell from my hand.

Panicked as if a flotilla of Vikings had just landed on our village shores, I sprinted screaming, arms flailing into the house.

Fear.

Fear everywhere.

Racquetballs.

Racquetballs everywhere in my glass head.

I ran through the downstairs, through all the rooms, looking for somewhere to hide. I was hyperventilating. No—I had to get out of the house. Bradley would sniff me out. The house was a prison. I had to get out. And not only that, I had to get rid of that *thing*... the robot. Who knew what Bradley would get up to with it. I had voted Republican in every election I was eligible for—as my mother did before her and hers before her when women were inadvisedly allowed to vote. The healing, power and goodness of Conservatism was in our blood. For the future of our marriage and for the future of American values I had to get rid of this fucking Sex fucking

Robot.

"Obamacare Sex Robot!" I screamed from the bottom of the stairs. "Bama-bot, get down here!"

The bedroom door upstairs opened. A naked mechanical facsimile of the Commander in Chief appeared at the head of the stairs, dong a-dangling. "Come over to my side of the aisle on that perineal massage finally?" it said.

"No! Garage! Now!"

"Affirmative, Holly."

I ran into the garage and the robot followed, bare feet padding across the tiled kitchen floor behind me.

"Get in!" I shouted, pointing at the box the robot came in. The Obamacare Sex Robot did as commanded. But as he sat down in it—and accompanied by the sounds of hydraulic gears spinning—began to fold himself into the folds of foam, I heard a car speeding down our street. *Oh God, oh God,* I thought, is that Bradley already?

I leaned over and yanked at the cover, helped shove the president's knees into the container. When he was finally in it I pulled at the box. It wouldn't budge. The robot looked at me quizzically. I grunted and pulled again but the box wouldn't move. What the hell was I thinking?

This robot weighed over two hundred pounds!

"Okay, get up! Help me with the box. Get up! Get out! Can you put it in the car?"

The robot looked at me. Seemed to be calculating something. Finally said, "Affirmative," and scampered out of the container.

The sound of the car got louder. Whoever it was, they were *flying*. I turned and saw Bradley's car roaring down our quaint suburban street, his dumb old *Outback* that he refused to trade in.

"Oh my God, hurry, hurry!" I shouted at the robot. I saw my phone on the floor and scooped it up.

Bradley swerved into our driveway and skidded to a stop.

The robot hoisted a corner of the box and struggled with it. The robot began dragging the box to the rear of the SUV.

The Outback driver's side door flew open. Bradley jumped out. The engine still running.

"Forget the box!" I shouted. "Forget it! Forget it!"

"Holly! Stop! Holly, stop what you're doing! I want to blow that robot! I command you to stop!"

"Jump in! Jump in the car, Obama!" I

49

screamed. I fumbled with the door. I turned to see Bradley running towards me up the driveway.

"Wanna blow it! Tickle th' taint!" Bradley yelled, almost upon me now. "Sucky sucky!"

I flung the door open and hopped inside.

Bradley's fingers scratched at my window as I pulled the door shut. He went for the handle, I pressed the lock.

With horror I looked over and realized in my haste that I'd locked out the *Bx-44* Gratification System too. The Commander in Chief doppelganger stared at me through the passenger window, a questioning look playing upon his mechanical face. I turned and met Bradley's eyes. He sneered, smiled and licked his lips.

"Come here, prezzie! Bwaddey likey!" shouted Bradley and took off around the front of the car.

When he was halfway around the hood, I unlocked the car doors and reached for the passenger door handle. But the Obama Sex Robot opened it, quicker than I'd seen anything move in my life, and jumped into the seat.

The door shut. I locked the car again.

Bradley made it around, but the president was safe inside. Bradley began pounding on the hood and the side of the Standard Utility Vehicle. He yanked at the side view mirror, twisting it around like an automotive titty twister, the psycho.

I was crying, scared, trembling. I fumbled with the fob and started up the car. I pressed the gas and the engine roared. At that exact moment, Bradley was in front of the hood. He looked with eye-wide fear at me.

We locked eyes. If I put the car in drive, I would have crushed him to death against the wall. Don't think I didn't think about it in the eons of that nanosecond. With all that happened later, I probably should have, and saved an entire nation a world of hurt. But I couldn't do it. I couldn't crush my husband to death between the hood of my SUV and the wall of our garage just because he was sex-crazed with lust for a governmental device that knew how to work the prostate like State Farm. I wasn't an animal. Yet.

But that doesn't mean I was a good driver either. I was still a woman.

I jammed the car in reverse and slammed on the gas and the SUV flew backwards. How had I forgotten about Bradley's shitty Subaru Outback sitting in the driveway?

CHAPTER FIVE

Bat Out of Heck

The SUV roared from the garage like the motorcycle on Meat Loaf's *Bat Out of Hell* album cover and crashed immediately into Bradley's car.

I screamed.

There was a nasty crunching and crinkling. The Obamacare Robot next to me sucked air through his teeth. (Did it need oxygen to survive? Also: I looked down and saw his still-erect penis rocking forward and backward like a pendulum from the impact.)

Not really thinking, I put the SUV in drive and sped off sideways across our front yard. Both the cyborg and I unconsciously put our seatbelts on. Looking quickly I saw that Bradley's Outback's airbags had deployed; Bradley wouldn't be able to drive after me. Which didn't stop me, of course, from crashing through our neighbors the Nabor's rustic, old-timey wooden fence and keep going. I wasn't exactly in my right frame of mind. We laid tracks on the Nabor's manicured, neon-emerald lawn, sped through a little grove of rosebushes and azaleas, chrysanthemums and bougainvillea, flowers exploding around us like a confetti cannon, then we were in a forest proper, where the deer and the deer ticks lived (thanks to our pernicious anti-hunting laws). The Lexus SUV shook, thudded and jumped violently between the trees as if we were reentering the atmosphere through an asteroid belt, like we were the motorcycle on Meat Loaf's *Bat Out of Hell II: Back Into Hell* record cover. Obama jumped up and down next to me, hopping in his seat like a piston. His head hit the ceiling a bunch. Penis flapping against his naked, perfectly-flat stomach of a teenager. Good Lord, was its dick actually getting *bigger* with all the jostling? Though my curiosity had been piqued, I was too scared to think about it with equanimity.

I screamed—the entire time. Blood-curdling, I tell you. I wasn't used to this daredevilry.

Soon we leaped a fallen log and passed out of the woods and skidded out onto a road diagonally.

The hood was smoking. I looked in both directions. No cars. I exhaled rapidly a hundred times. I was hyperventilating.

The Obamacare Robot put its hand on my stomach. It was freezing cold.

"How—?"

"A fetus will react to cold."

"Get your—!"

Then I felt my baby kick. Two quick thuds against my uterus. Kick! Kick! I looked at the Obamacare Robot.

"I just wanted to make sure your unborn child was okay through all that intense vehicular lurching and jolting," The robot said. "Your heart rate is rapid, but the fetus' is within normal parameters. Healthy."

Satisfied, the machine leaned back in the passenger seat and looked out the front window, plain as day, as if enjoying an after-church Sunday drive.

I was dumbfounded. Also angry.

"Robot! Don't you *ever*..." I didn't know what to say. I faltered. What was I feeling? Looking down, I saw the erection still there, the mechanical man's penis still incredibly large, twitching like a stallion on steroids. I didn't like the way the back of my mind was reacting to it, a sultry smoke of hormones swirling in the mists of my mind's eye. If I couldn't honestly be angry over the machine caring about the welfare of my child, I could still at least be angry about *that*. "Look, robot. Can you put your *thing* away please? I don't want to look at it, anymore."

"This? Yes, Mrs. McQuerty." And the hard cock dwindled down to a normal size—probably still a chubby, but the back of my mysterious mind could at least handle a chubby in the vicinity.

"Thank you." I did a three point turn. *Thank you? Why did I just say thank you to a fascist robot,* I thought to myself as I put the car in drive and drove down the road, away from my house. As away as possible.

Minutes later we were out of town (I prayed out of range of Bradley's gaydar) and it was then that I realized I had no plan.

"Where can I return you? Do you know?" I asked.

"Return? Does not compute."

"You came from somewhere, right? I want—need—to bring you back there. My sanity demands it."

"Apologies, but I am only aware of booting up in your garage. That is my first memory."

"But where did you come from? Where were you built?"

"Built? Hold. This *Bx-44 Gratification Unit*, Serial Number 34377-2288 was fabricated in Pueblo, Colorado with parts manufactured in Xian-Dung Province, China. Designed by Apple in Cupertino, California. Approved by federal mandate in Washington, District of Columbia."

"Great. Okay. But is there a repository or something? How about just the Post Office?"

Before the cyborg of pleasure could answer, my phone rang. It was my mother. I answered it and immediately starting blubbering. I wasn't even sure if I was saying English words or words in any language for that matter, unless you count female nonsensical noise as language. The SUV began swerving back and forth across the road. I didn't care if I hit a tree. I was inconsolable.

When there was a lull in my blubber, my mother cut in, her voice smooth and motherly. "Holly, honey. Bradley told me everything. Just go back home dear."

"Okay."

"Just go home and all will be forgiven."

"Okay… Wait. What? He told you… *everything?*"

"Yes, honey. Honey, just go home. Bradley is waiting. Your sweet Bradley is waiting for you to come home. You bring that sick robot back and then return it back to the government."

Something about that didn't seem right—didn't make sense. I didn't see Bradley admitting to my mother that he was a secret bottom-boy and was sex-crazed for the Dark Lord President of the United States. "What did he tell you?" I asked.

"Oh… I'd really rather not repeat it."

"Please, mother."

There was a moment of silence. I could hear my mother breathing heavy. Then she spoke. And she spoke utter insanity: "That he caught you using the… the… *thing.* The Gratification, um, System. That he came home from the gym and you were laying with it, as the Bible says—oh, Holly, *really!*"

"What!" I screamed into the phone.

"Holly, honey, please don't shout. Your mother's ears aren't what they used to be, but I can hear you just fine."

"That lying *scumbag!* I caught *him* with it. And do you know who it looks like? Can you guess who the sex robot looks like? You're never going to believe it! It looks exactly like a very, very famous black man that everyone hates! Care to venture a guess who? The most powerful man in the world? Need a better hint?"

"Oh, Holly, don't be ri*dic*ulous."

"It's true!"

Her voice got stern. "I'm sorry, but that's just *too* much. Honestly, where could you come up with a story like that? And I don't think anyone at the club would believe a story like that either. I mean, Bradley—he's such a *man's* man. Have you seen his body? The clothes he wears. Oh, honey, you'd be stupid to give that up."

"What do you mean, give it up?"

"And live in sin with an Government Sex Robot."

Out of the corner of my eye I saw a flash of red. "Was that a stop sign?" I asked the naked robot next to me.

I hung up the phone. Not because of what my mother was saying, though it was bitchily insensitive—but because suddenly there were flashing lights in my rearview mirror…

CHAPTER SIX

Helpful Assessments of Possible Dangerous or Life-Threatening Situations For Licensee of Medical Sexual Assistant Robot Come Standard With Affordable Care Act Package

"Fuck, fuck, fuck! That was a stop sign, wasn't it?"

"Yes," replied the *Bx-44.*

"Fuck, fuck, fuck!"

"Fuck, fuck, fuck!" repeated the robot in my same hectic tone of voice. I looked at him. His face was as placid as ever. The most placid, most irritating Obama-face it could have mustered to get under my skin.

"Why did you just say what I just said?" I asked.

"Attempting empathy."

"Well, it's not working." I was still driving. I'd slowed down, but I certainly hadn't stopped yet. The cop behind me started playing different, more urgent sirens. The road, hedged in by bright green woods on either side warped in my vision—how easy it would be slam on the gas and disappear down the road like Alice through the rabbit hole.

My toe tickled the gas.

"The top speed of a Lexus LX 570 SUV is 137 miles per hour. The top speed of a Dodge Charger, the make of the vehicle currently following us, even without standard law enforcement modification, exceeds 150 miles per hour."

"Where did *that* come from?"

"Helpful assessments of possible dangerous or life-threatening situations for licensee of medical sexual assistant robot come standard with Affordable Care Act package."

"Okay, okay! Dammit. Get in the back. Climb in the back. No—the *way* back. Hide. Thank God this car has tinted windows. You've got to *hide*. Duck down back there and *stay quiet*."

I pulled into the parking lot of a strip mall. It

was completely vacant. All the businesses in the area of course had closed down because of Barack Obama's Plan for America. The place was spooky, eerily quiet—silence like a creeping moss. There had been a florists, a Game Stop, a Subway Sandwiches, a VCR repair shop, a Papa Gino's and a bookstore. All gone now. Never to return and sell stuff. What makes America America was the exchange of goods and services, and Obama had ruined it. Then he sprayed the country with sex robots.

The cop hopped out of his car and stormed up to my window. He was pissed. I rolled my window down. "Anything wrong office—"

"Care to explain why you failed to pull over!?"

"Well, I… aren't—"

"Are you stupid or do you not know what you're supposed to do when a police officer flashes his lights behind you?"

"I'm a woman. Alone. I was told to drive to somewhere public, just in case it was someone impersonating an officer. Something like that. I'm sorry, but I'm a woman. As you can see."

The cop frowned. But it seemed to take the edge off. "Do you know why I pulled you over?"

"Yes. Unfortunately I do. The stop sign. I'm

sorry. It was a mistake."

"You seem nervous. Is something the matter?"

"No. No, I'm just—I've never been pulled over before, that's all."

"Ma'am, you were driving recklessly and the back of your car is all messed up. Do you care about the safety of your community?"

"Of course…"

Suddenly there was a noise in the back of the car. A person moving: the squeak of skin on leather.

The police officer and I met eyes. In that infinity of a second, I saw the cop grow alarmed, his training taking over. He peered past me into the back seat.

"Is that—? And… and… *naked?*" The cop's elbow on his gun side bent a bit.

"Good day, officer," the Obamacare Sex Robot said from the back seat. The dumb thing hadn't actually gotten in the far back behind the seats like I'd meant, just the back seats. "Would you care for a bit of loving this fine spring day? Perhaps a fantasy revolving around the misuse of authority? I am told my reacharounds are the bomb diggity."

The gun was out. The officer screaming. He took a step back. "Get out of the car! Out of the car, now! Mr. President, how did you get here? Were you kidnapped?"

"No! No!" I yelled, "That's not my president! Not *the* president, I mean!"

"Out!" the cop yelled. He lunged forward. With his free hand he reached inside the car, popped the handle and flung it open. Then he grabbed me by the hair and yanked. I fell from the car onto the road.

"Unhand her, officer!" I was face down, and handcuffs were being doffed, but before I knew what was happening, the *Bx-44 Gratification System* had exited the SUV on the other side and ran around the car. "Unhand Mrs. McQuerty, for she is with child!" the Commander in Chief lookalike commanded again.

"What the—?"

Before the policeman could do anything, the Sex Robot had his hands on him. The Barackbot lifted the policeman from the ground. Held him by the neck. "Mr. President, Mr. Presid—" the cop implored, face going red.

The robot threw the cop twenty feet into the woods, caterwauling. He landed with a poof of sticks and leaves. You know the sound—when animal meat and vegetable meet.

The Obamacare Sex Robot eased me from the pavement. "Are you okay?" it asked and I nodded. "Good! No time!" He picked me up and with utmost speed and care placed me back up in the driver's seat. He jumped through the rear door.

I slammed on the gas. Pedal to the metal. My door slammed shut and I laid rubber as the SUV blasted down the road.

Bullets tore into the back of the truck. That cop was actually shooting at me! I couldn't believe it! Pop! Pop! Pop! What the fuck! Did he actually think that I had the President naked in the back seat of my car? Wouldn't he have heard something about that on his walkie-talkie—oh, I don't know: a missing dang POTUS? Wouldn't he have been afraid of shooting the president?

I was crying. I was shaking. There was no going back now. This was serious shit.

We sped off into the hinterlands of Connecticut.

And into the bomb diggity.

Chapter Seven
The Warmth of the Poor

Hours later I was exhausted. It was night. I could drive no further and had serious reservations about letting the Sex Robot take the wheel, though it made many attestations to the fact that it was a fully licensed driver—as well as masseuse, midwife and man-whore.

We drove by a rundown motel for poor people. Perfect. I pulled in the parking lot.

Maybe some sleep would clear my head. I could figure out what the hell to do tomorrow morning. Maybe Bradley would come to his senses. I couldn't believe how hard he'd lied to my mother. But then again, it would have been supremely embarrassing for him if the truth got out. And therefore embarrassing for me. Could I deal with it? Deal with Bethany's barbs? I'd be getting ragged on from here to eternity, I knew. People would whisper, at the club, at the super market, at the gun range, at the beach house on the Cape, at the beach house on the Vineyard. Did he think that I'd really want the truth out there? That I'd tell everyone about what I'd seen—as if I didn't want to wash the whole sordid scene from my brain? Then I remembered Bradley in the garage. He was like a sex maniac, an engorged tick ready to blow (dong), frothing at the mouth. What had gotten into him (besides the hard, glistening cock of the prez, I mean)? Yeah, we'd had a few financial setbacks, but we were still well off I thought. We had tons of stocks still, our family money, inheritances, our trust funds and mutual funds at home and offshore—everything else the Obama administration hadn't managed to steal from hardworking Americans yet.

Thankfully, I had my gym clothes still in the back of the Lexus. The Sex Robot looked silly in them—a pink sweatshirt and sweatpants—but not as silly as a naked black person walking from the car to the room would have been.

I booked a room, made sure no one was around and we went inside quickly.

Immediately, I sat down on the side of the bed and fell apart. I began to sob. Full-bodied earthquakes rocked my crevasses. I leaned over and put my face in my hands.

And then.

"Are you okay?" the Obamacare Sex Robot that looked exactly like the real Democratic President Barack Obama said. "You seem tense. Would you like a massage?" And he slid both hands along my shoulders. He was kneeling behind me on the bed.

I shuddered.

"Get the—!" I started to shout, anger boiling up from my throat. But in an instant, Obama Robot's palms had conformed to the shape of my shoulders like a mold, his thumbs making small circles on my upper back. It felt heavenly; I needed not finish my statement…

The cyborg's hands were warm, soothing. He had already found the ache in my shoulders where my stress collected. (It would take Bradley hours to find this hidden pool of knotted muscles—and endless cajoling just to get him to give me a massage.) Using his fingers, the Obamacare Sex Robot worked my muscles, going deeper and deeper. I exhaled, the stress evaporating from my body on fluffy wings.

"Wow, that's…" I trailed off. I closed my eyes. It was the first nice thing a man had done for me in a long, long time.

"I know this time of pregnancy is stressful for you," Obama said. "But motherhood is a beautiful thing. It's hard work, yes, but the most beautiful work there is. Beautiful, just like you, Holly McQuerty of 18 Maple Lane, Barndale Heights, Connecticut. Here, lean your head forward."

I did as commanded. Mr. Obama lifted my hair up gently and moved it to the side. He began trailing his fingers up and down the small ribbon-like muscles in my neck, working the tiny edges of each tendon and muscle. It felt like heaven, have I already mentioned that? Obama 2000 here had the fingertips of *an angel*. With each wonderful stroke, relaxation flooded down my spine and, radiating out throughout my back, turned it to jelly.

Soon I was *very* warm.

I mmmed with pleasure; my head lolled on my shoulders. "That feels amazing," I groaned slowly, letting it all out. "I didn't realize how stressed out I've been."

"Would you like to lie down on the bed?"

Wait, what did *that* mean? Was this robot trying to seduce me, to sex me, to Bradley me? I came out of my massage-induced reverie, suddenly aware again of what was happening. Perhaps the Obamacare Sex Robot sensed this new tension in my body though, because next he said: "I just want to be able to massage your back fully, Holly. It is difficult this way, while you are sitting up, to get at all of your stress points. I can feel knots here... and here..." he said, digging his thumb into my lower back.

I opened my mouth in silent scream. *Whoa.* It hurt but it was the good kind of hurt. "Ohhhhhh..." I moaned. "Okay. Let me lie down. Is it okay with my stomach though?"

"Here let me adjust the pillows."

Robo-bama took the pillows and made a circle with them, a nest with a hole in the middle for my bump. I stretched out and lay down on it. A perfect fit.

Now the *real* massage began.

First, The Obama set the mood. He turned off the overhead fluorescents. Then he turned on the little lamp on the nightstand. He draped my scarf over it, bathing the room in soft, amber light. A flick of a button on the clock radio and smooth, tropical music from an AM channel bathed the room in soft, amber sound.

Then the robot touched my back. To start with, he ran his fingertips up and down slowly, just the lightest of touches from the base of my neck to my lumbar region. This engaged my skin. It rippled with anticipation. "Mmm, that feels nice," I mouthed into the bed.

"Good," he said and pressed harder. I groaned. With his palms he pressed into my body. He massaged circles large and small into my muscles for what seemed like hours.

I began to drift. To float along on clouds of relaxation. Gay husband? What gay husband? On the run from the law? What law? In a dirt motel? What dirt motel? Sexual inhibitions? What sexual inhibitions?

Uh-oh.

It was a moment of weakness, that's all. That's all I can say about it. The robot massage... it weakened me. I had been through so much that day. A strong American woman can only take so much.

So I decided to take a little more.

Chapter Eight
Blasphemy is the Hottest Aphrodisiac

It was naughty. It was dirty. I didn't care. I wanted it. Whatever it was. Bring it.

Maybe it was the atmosphere of the motel: gross. A hideout for poor people. I couldn't imagine who would need this motel in the middle of nowhere. There weren't any attractions within miles. It was just a rundown, one-story string of rooms by the side of a country highway.

And then I thought, how easy it would be to sink into this life. The life of the poor and miserable. To sink into the mud, like a mud bath. Accepting the truth that there was no room for advancement, no need to pay club dues, no brutal clawing to the top of the social ladder. Just not fighting the mud, just letting go—just taking those government welfare handouts and not

71

caring, and then doing it, and doing it, and doing it on the government's dime, like some kind of filthy heedless wild animal.

Using my little groans of assent as guides, the Obamacare Sex Robot work its way lower and lower on my back.

Soon it was rubbing my butt. It felt amazing. The knuckles worked my hipbones, dug in real deep into the flesh of my ass. He grabbed each cheek in his hand and rolled them in circles, first one way, then the next.

Keeping one hand on a cheek to hold me down, pressing my hips harder into the bed, the robot rolled the other hand down my hamstrings. I had no idea I was tense here too. But the feeling was darling. The Obama robot discovered worries I didn't know I had and scattered them away.

I lifted my butt up off the bed ever so slightly. Then I reached down and slowly lifted the hem of my dress. I did nothing different—my head face down in the pillow—except move my skirt up.

In a minute the dress was up over my hips. "It's better if you work the skin directly, right?" I whispered into the mattress.

"Yes," was the robot's only answer, in Barack Obama's voice, but passed through a Speak & Spell.

And then it moved its fingers along the back of my legs, starting from down at the feet and working up. It tickled the skin along the way, gentle butterfly kisses, fluttering by. The sensation was hair-raising. Hot. So hot. My body responded with a wave of heat. I felt myself get wetter between my legs.

I raised my ass a little bit more off the bed, the better for access, if the robot decided to take things further, and spread my legs a little more, I would only acquiesce. I would not go out of my way to be touched in my privates by this thing. But if it wanted me, it wanted me. That's what I was telling myself.

If the device was a medical device, and knew what was best, I would not fight the diagnosis.

Then I felt it.

The robot had reached my perky bottom. It slid two fingers under the edges of my panties and began working my cheeks again. With just a simple finger on each cheek, the massage was masterful, diving deep into the hidden realms of dark muscles in my glutes. It relaxed and soothed me, but, and it should go with out saying now, started to turn me on. I was getting hot and bothered.

Now its fingers converged at the center, just below my ass and just above my womanly hole, that thin land of flesh, where a million times more nerve endings meet the skin. An invasion. A home invasion. But I allowed it. Threw the house key down to the robber on the porch. The thing's fingers rubbed back and forth, in little circles and shapes. First it was tiny shivers, then shakes, then full-on shudders.

"God!" I screamed.

I writhed. Whatever secret button in me he pressed there, a ribbon of pleasure unfurled up my back. It felt like I suddenly had angel wings.

I couldn't take it anymore!

The ache was too strong.

"Touch me, robot. Finger my pussy." I moaned.

Oh God, the heat.

"Yes, Holly," replied the cyborg.

The Obamacare Sex Robot took those two fingers and hooked them around the hem of my panties. With one long, slow motion he dragged them down my legs. The dusty motel air touched my naked ass and pussy and I felt as one with the place. Like a dirty commoner, doing whatever perversions floated my boat, like a drunk ape, drunk on cheap wine.

And now like a dirt-person's Jet Ski, pleasure invaded my pond, loud, misty-wet, bouncing on waves.

The robot began caressing my outer lips.

"Ooh," I oohed.

"Good?" the robot asked.

"No. *Bad*. So bad, so *very* bad…" I moaned. I had a brief worry that the robot would take this the wrong way, that it would stop, but my fears were assuaged.

"Who's a… *bad* girl?" it asked.

"Oh, mmm, me," I whispered.

The robot slid a finger inside my pussy. My breath quickened. My heart began to pound in my chest. What was this? Why was I doing this?

"Oh my God," I said.

The robot slipped his finger inside me, stretching my lips. It had been so long and I was so incredibly tight. He slid it in deeper. And deeper. He slid it out, and the feeling a mix of pleasure and agony. Agony because I wanted it so bad. So very bad. I was a bad girl. Letting the man

I hated the most in the world inside me, inside my privates. He slid it in and out and I clenched around his finger, wanting to keep it inside me forever, this doppelganger's dirty dark digit.

Now his other dark finger found my clitoris. Within seconds he found the pattern and motion that pleasured me fastest and hardest. Little circles at the top of my sexy little button, then long strides down the lips framing the front of my hole.

I was wetter than I'd ever been.

My pussy was wetter than a wetback crossing the Rio Grande.

"Ooh, Obama," I cooed. "What are you doing to me? Are you touching me? Why are fingering me like that?"

"Because you're the most beautiful woman in the world. Your feminine hips, your long, luscious brown hair. Your little nose and round cheeks. I have no needs other than to make you happy, Holly."

I nearly came at these words. Nearly. It surged up and then surged back. But the orgasm was coming. The coming was on its way. The coming was coming. Fast. Suddenly it was here again. "Holy shit!" I screamed.

My throat began shuddering moans. They came deep from within me, somewhere dark like the bottom of a well or a cave, filled with good luck pennies. My body started shaking. I'd never felt such sweeping pleasure. It was bipartisan. It had gathered together in my hips and announced itself far and wide across my body like a countryside yodeler.

The Obamacare Sex Robot worked my hole like a master, like a kung-fu master but not for kung-fu but for my dripping wet pussy. He was infiltrating my pussy like a ninja. My pussy opened itself up to the assassination. Little tiny karate chops, back and forth across my clit, which had hardened with the abuse, multiplied tenfold throughout the kingdom of my body. While that was going on, the other finger slid in and out of my cunt, faster and faster, dripping wet now, my pussy juices soaking the disgusting blue blanket on the bed underneath my writhing body.

Then Obama did something so bold. So audacious. He pinched my clit, held it in place, imprisoned the pussy, and then slid the other finger up, and curled it around inside me towards the front, to a bumpy patch of flesh hidden even from me. It was lovely, dark and deep. He pressed my insides, squeezed them together and everything fell apart. He destroyed me.

I let go of all of my preconceived notions of what a climax was…

Pleasure exploded inside my pussy like the rocket's red light!

"Oh God!"

Fireworks. My hips shook, my entire body shook. The poor-person motel around us disappeared, the fake wood-paneled walls fell away and suddenly we were in the Taj Mahal, a big white palace, open, spread open as much as I was. It was a palace of pleasure, we were kings and queens, we were royalty—royally coming. My orgasm blinded me and deafened me. Somewhere in this great white hall I heard a voice, it was wordlessly screaming in pleasure, barely containing itself, coming apart at the seams, hoarse and rough and wow—I realized that voice was *mine*.

Then I came back to reality and I was still coming, still moaning in ecstasy in the dingy motel room on a bed probably a dozen people had overdosed on. My uterus contracted tight around my stomach. My inner walls shook. My whole body was an earthquake. Hormones going haywire. A liberal robot had dirtied my body—and it felt liberating. Blasphemy is the hottest aphrodisiac.

And well… Okay.

I'll admit it.

But only to you, dear reader, and no one else. If the truth got out it could ruin my reputation, and we *can't* have that. A woman has such little else.

So let me tell you…

It was the greatest orgasm I'd ever had.

And it was all thanks to Obamacare.

Special Preview of Book Two in the
My Obamacare Nightmare Series
by Lacey Noonan

The Blacker the Robot the Moister the Oyster
Falling for the Obamacare Sex Robot

CHAPTER ONE
Suddenly Bethany

I awoke, happier than I'd awoken in a long time. The orgasm—*good Lord that orgasm!*—had freed me like Abraham Lincoln. I'd fallen asleep blubbering, the color of amber in my eyes, yellow and joyous. And sweet dreams had bathed me in their happy glows all night.

On dwindling waves of pleasure, I rode the Sea of Nod, until my sleepy ship had touched the sandy bottom of morning.

Man, that doppelganger was a doozy of a

fingerbanger. What other delights awaited me, I thought... but only fleetingly, for I dared not think of where this naughtiness headed.

I stretched and smiled. Even the bump had slept well inside me. Nary a karate chop all night. I rolled over and was surprised to see the Obamacare Sex Robot sitting in a chair, still wearing my pink sweatsuit, staring straight ahead quietly. Strange. It would take some time to get used to that. Of course the machine didn't need to sleep, possibly just reboot whenever Microsoft Excel crashed inside it or something.

The robot turned to me and smiled its not-quite-right, robotic smile, some kind of digital ropes and pulleys lifting the sides of its mouth and showing its porcelain teeth to me in accordance with the scene its optical sensors sensed and it algorithms' response to it. Weird. I forgot that it was weird. Which kind of bummed me out...

Oh my God, what the *hell* was I doing!

I sat up quickly in bed.

On the run from the law... from my husband, from my mother. And shacking up with an Obama thingie. An Obama! Guilt oozed in around the edges of my mind like a black oil. I started to feel low, so very low in the body and spirit.

But then a quiver of remembrance shook my vagina like an aftershock. And the feelings of the night whispered across my mind. It was pussy-joy pure and good and God damn if that ain't the cat's pajamas.

Wow, right?

The thoughts came fast and loose: Who cared if it was by a dumb Democrat robot? A woman's pussy is apolitical. Just beat the pussy up and you can count on *my* vote. (I don't think politicians, males especially, talk about pussies, vaginas, hoohas and women in general enough in the halls of power, tbh.) Shoot, it wasn't so bad, getting molested by a D-Crat—my body didn't know what rocked it, only that it had been rocked and rocked like a hurricane.

Still, I needed distraction. "Turn on the TV or something, will you?" I said.

The TV was one of those old square shitboxes with fake brown wood on the side, sitting on a cart, facing the bed. The robot turned a knob. The TV flicked on. I was surprised that it worked. And that it actually picked up CNN. The advertisement for "Free Cable" on the decrepit sign out front wasn't false advertising.

What was on CNN, however, was horrifying.

"—bring you now to Connecticut with breaking news. A local police officer has been attacked by Barack Obama. That's right, you heard right. By President Barack Obama himself."

I shot up in bed.

On the TV, to the left of the reporter, they played blurry footage on a loop. It was from a different angle than I'd experienced it, but it most certainly was footage from the day before. My traffic stop. It was the police officer's point of view. The naked Obamacare Sex Robot whisks around my SUV and hoists the cop in the air. A blur of green and white is all that is shown while the police officer flies through the air. He must have been wearing a body camera. "Beryl Furnette is on the scene. We go there now, live. Hi Beryl."

"Hi, Taffy."

"Any word on who the woman in the vehicle with President Obama is?"

"Not yet, Taffy. Authorities are staying mum. Though we do know that assaulting a police officer is a felony and carries with it a mandatory minimum of a lifetime prison sentence. And kidnapping of the president, which is treason, carries with it another five hundred hours of community service."

"This is insane," I said to the robot. "Why don't they confirm with the actual president that you're not the actual president! This is nuts! Where is the actual president? Typical fucking CNN drumming up fervor without due diligence! A bitching birch tree has more journalistic integrity than liberal-ass media CNN! Fuck!"

And then there it was: my face on the TV. A freeze frame of me sitting in my SUV, while I was talking to the police officer. Anyone who knew me would recognize me instantly from the photo. It was only a matter of time before the police found out. Maybe they already knew. Maybe they were already on the way here. I'd used my credit card to book the room last night like a stupid idiot. Stupid, stupid, stupid!

"Taffy, police are trying to track down the identity of this woman. They are not sure how she managed to kidnap and brainwash the president into protecting her, but there it is."

"CNN!" I screamed. "What the shit is this???????"

Suddenly, yes so very *suddenly*...

There was a knock at the door. I screamed with fright and pulled the covers up to my chin.

"Would you like me to answer the door, Holly?" the Obamacare *Bx-44* Sex Robot asked.

"No!" I hissed. "And lower your voice."

"Would you like me to answer the door, Holly?" the robot said again, at the same exact, infuriating volume, only in a deeper register, like Barry White.

The person knocked again. Louder this time.

"What do we do what do we do?" I said.

"Answer a door that is knocked upon?" the robot ventured.

"Are you crazy?"

"I am a robot. I am neither sane nor insane. I merely perform preordained functions, primarily in the industries of hospitality, but also self-defense and midwifery and husbandry."

"What if it's the police here to arrest us? I can't been seen with an Obamacare Sex Robot! Especially one that *looks* like Obama! I can't! Obama's a Socialist Nazi-Crat Demtard! We have to get out somehow."

"Who is this 'Obama' you keep mentioning?" The Obamacare Sex Robot asked. "Is it some kind of Gaelic mispronunciation of the state of

Alabama?"

"What? You don't know who Obama is? What the hell? *How?*"

The door knocked again.

"Oh God, oh God, oh God. Okay. Creep to the door and see who it is through the peephole."

But before Obama could creep like a creep to the peep, I heard Bethany's voice. "Holly!" she whisper-yelled, "Holly! Are you in there? It's me, Beth!" She rapped again on the door.

How the fuck did Bethany find us? My dumb friend Bethany. This was crazy. Not just crazy, but like cray-cray level crazy. Did Brad squeal on me or had she already seen the news this morning? Bethany wasn't exactly Miss Up-To-Date on the latest goings on. Whatever news managed to slink through the cracks in *US Weekly* like a slinky dress on Kate Moss was all she knew about. Kardashian-Stefani-Anniston this and that.

"Should I answer the door, Holly?" Obama asked.

"No! Ssh!" I whispered at him.

The robot froze midstride.

A few moments passed, more pregnant than my fat ass.

Silence, scary cray-cray silence.

Finally, I heard Bethany walk away. A minute later she was knocking on the door next over. I heard a person mumble inside the room, cough up a menthol-ravaged lung a bunch, then answer the door. Within seconds there was shouting, screaming, scuffling. It sounded like low-class chaos.

This was my chance!

"Come on, Obama!" I shouted.

I heaved myself from the bed, threw on my shoes, pulled up my panties and shimmied my dress down over my hips.

The scuffle next door seemed to intensify. Whatever was happening out there, Bethany would surely be occupied by it.

I squinted through the peephole. Couldn't see anything. I snatched my fob from the dresser and unlocked the SUV in front of the room while we were still inside. I looked through the peephole again...

The coast was clear.

"Let's go!" I yelled.

The door flung open and me and the sex robot bolted for the car!

Dear Reader,

As a purveyor of the written word, I survive on interaction with my readers. If you have the time and enjoyed any part of what you just read, please review this book anywhere you see fit: Amazon, Goodreads, twitter, whatever!

It's the 90's now... Reviews and word of mouth on the internet are truly the life's blood of any writer. And I love hearing from readers. So tell me what you think!

Thanks again and happy reading,
xoxo
Lacey

ABOUT THE AUTHOR

Well, let me tell you about good ol' Lacey Noonan. Lacey lives on the east coast with her family. When not sailing, sampling fine whiskeys or making veggie tacos, she loves to read and write steamy, strange, silly, psychological and sexy stories. During daylight hours she is a web designer and developer, but mostly a mom.

For more information on Lacey Noonan, why not point your browser snake at:

Amazon Author Profile
amazon.com/author/laceynoonan

Mailing List
http://eepurl.com/bEeNgv

Facebook
facebook.com/laceynoonan123

Twitter
twitter.com/laceynoonan

Email
laceynoonan123@gmail.com

OTHER BOOKS BY *Lacey Noonan*

THE BLACKER THE ROBOT THE MOISTER THE OYSTER: FALLING FOR THE OBAMACARE SEX ROBOT (MY OBAMACARE NIGHTMARE BOOK 2)

The saga continues! Holly wakes up in a dirt person motel in the middle of nowhere with her runaway Obamacare Sex Robot, half-naked, sweaty with bliss. It was a brief moment of respite in a dangerous chase, but soon they're at it again, taking a cool, relaxing swim in a high-risk pool. Soon the water is churning around them with a pleasure that daresn't speak its name. (I'm talking what happens when bodies start slapping, people.) And then things heat up even hotter than that when Death Panel Goons surround Holly and her electronic lover, threatening everything just when she's decided her life is finally back on track.

SEDUCED BY THE DAD BOD: BOOK ONE IN THE CHILL DAD SUMMER HEAT SERIES

Amanda's back from college for the summer, sexy and bored. Mr. Baldwin is a chill dad who loves swimming, singing '90s hits, Super Soakers and has a body like a big sack of wet sugar. What happens when these two star-crossed lovers cross paths? And oh yeah—he's her boyfriend's dad? Uh-oh! By turns devastatingly erotic and incisive, this first installment of Lacey Noonan's hot new summery Dad Bod saga will leave you questioning everything in your life.

Hot Boxed:
How I Found Love on Amazon

Hot Boxed is the story of Randi, a 20-something girl working at an Amazon Distribution Center who wants more out of life. Assuming she'll work there forever, a name pops up on her scanner that ignites her passions. Does she have the courage to break the chains that bind her, to step out of her dreary life and do something so, so, so crazy to get what she wants? Find out in this super-steamy story!

The Nasty Woman's Guide to
Deplorable Baskets

Here is the most comprehensive book on baskets ever published. Guiding you on your baskety journey are the Ladies of the New England Basket Weavers Association. An energetic bunch, they are as varied as the baskets they weave. Some weave as a hobby. Some weave to put food on the table. Some are old. Some are young. But all of them are complete bitches. It's up to you to decide who is who and who will survive the inevitable grudge-match and battle of egos which will more than likely tear the fabric of the club apart like a pack of nasty wolves. So hop aboard the Basket Train. Next stop: Baskets! As Madge Beaverworth says in her wonderful introduction: "Baskets, baskets, baskets!"

I Don't Care if my Best Friend's Mom is a Sasquatch, She's Hot and I'm Taking a Shower With Her… Because It's the New Millennium

Life for Jason is one wild experience after another. But then one night, a chance encounter dredges up a long-forgotten mystery, and suddenly he is trapped on a roller coaster of wildness. Is it more wildness than he can handle? Now he is on the run with his star-crossed lover. Will they reach a shower in time, or will the natural heat that burns within her consume them both? Literally, the steamiest book you will read all year!

I Don't Care If My Sasquatch Lover Says the World is Exploding, She's Hot But I Play Bass and There's Nothing Hotter Right Now Than Rap-Rock (…Because It's the New Millennium • Book Two)

Star-crossed lovers Jason and Starla are back in this devastatingly sexy and fun sequel. On the run from the devious Lemaire family and lost in the woods for weeks looking for the rendezvous that will get them to Starla's homeland, they are at their wits end when Jason abruptly joins the rap-rock band 311 (currently on tour with the Lilith Fair), throwing their whirlwind romance—and their very lives—into jeopardy. Welcome to the new millennium! Or is it?

THE BABYSITTER ONLY RINGS ONCE

This is NOT your typical babysitter story... One night when Sophie realizes she's left something scandalous at the Lindstrom's—the affluent family she has babysat for years now—she goes against all the fibers of her being and decides to get it back—no matter what, even if it means more scandal. Find out what Sophie recovers in this seriously HOT and suspenseful story by Lacey Noonan.

EAT FRESH: FLO, JAN & WENDY AND THE FIVE DOLLAR FOOTLONG

"God damn, marketing events are bitch." And so begins the sexy, wild adventures of our three protagonists, Jan, Flo and Wendy—the three hottest stars of the contemporary TV commercial scene. After a fight with Wendy's agent, the girls take it upstairs to Flo's VIP hotel room, where they soon discover the pleasures of each other's bodies—as well as the very valuable, last remaining Five Dollar Footlong at the event. Caution: Hottt!

A Gronking to Remember: Book One in the Rob Gronkowski Erotica Series

Leigh has a serious problem. And it's driving a "spike" between her and her husband Dan. When she accidentally witnesses the NFL's biggest wrecking ball, Rob Gronkowski of the New England Patriots, do his patented "Gronk Spike," she is suddenly hornier than she's ever been. This causes her to go on a rampage of her own—a rampage of "self-discovery." And soon everyone's lives have changed. Romance! Sports!

A Gronking to Remember 2: Chad Goes Deep in the Neutral Zone (Book Two in the Rob Gronkowski Erotica Series)

The saga continues! When Leigh spurns his advances at a party he throws in her honor, Dan's friend Chad kidnaps her, stealing her away to his personal New England Patriots Shangri-La, a secret Man Cave hundreds of feet below sea level he affectionately calls his "Chadmiral's Quarters." There she learns about a side of Gronk she'd never known, changing her life forever. Secrets will be revealed—Gronktastic secrets. Possibly the greatest sequel ever written. Makes the original look like a certified *piece of shit!*

A Cruzmas Carol: Ted Cruz Takes a Dickens of a Constitutional

Ted Cruz is *done* with politics. He's throwing himself a sex-fueled, drunken bacchanal and then he's joining the private sector. But his plans are about to change. After a hot makeout sesh with his sexy staffer Roberta, Ted has a digestive emergency and sprints to the men's room, where he runs into an old, long-dead coworker. Irritated, not heeding this magical spirit's warnings, Ted is told he will be visited by three more ghosts before the night is over. And so within minutes Ted is being sucked through glory hole after ol' glory hole to the past, present and future to learn some heartwarming lessons about America, freedom and also American freedom.

Shipwrecked on the Island of the She-Gods: A South Pacific Trans Sex Adventure

Shipwrecked on the Island of the She-Gods is a seriously sexually-charged adventure of heart-pounding exotica that doesn't skimp on story or skimpily-clad native girls with "a little something extra." And it's a little something extra that Noah, Julian and Owen will experience over and over in the steamy jungle, along the shores and atop towering mountains until they're begging for mercy. And then begging for more.

THE HOTNESS: FIVE
BURNING HOT NOVELLAS

PREPARE TO BE TURNED THE HELL ON. Here are five novellas that will titillate and drive you wild, running the gamut of erotic fantasies. If you've ever wanted all of Lacey Noonan's books in one easy, accessible place for one low price, then this is the book for you, sexy-pants. Contains the novellas: *Submitting the Landlord; Hot Boxed: How I Found Love on Amazon; The Babysitter Only Rings Once; I Don't Care if My Best Friend's Mom is a Sasquatch, She's Hot and I'm Taking a Shower With Her (...Because It's the New Millennium);* and *Eat Fresh: Flo, Jan & Wendy and the Five Dollar Footlong.*

Made in the USA
San Bernardino, CA
02 April 2018